Miracles and Blessings

Patricia Spratley

First Edition.

Publisher: Living With More Publications

Cover Design: Allyson Edits, Allyson Deese

This work is based on a true story. Names, places, and some events have been changed to protect the innocent and the privacy of those even remotely connected to the story. Any song lyrics and titles have been properly cited within the text.

Scriptures were taken from the HOLY BIBLE: King James Version, New International Version and the Message Bible.

ISBN: 978-0-578-42375-3

AUTHOR'S CONTACT INFO

Email:
spratleypatricia@yahoo.com

Facebook:
Author Patricia Spratley

From the Heart of the Author

I would like to dedicate this book to the people who are addicted to drugs and alcohol; to those who are walking the streets late at night jumping in and out of cars - prostituting. I would also like to dedicate this book to people that are suffering from kidney failure and hate getting up and going to dialysis. God knows and sees all. Hang on in there, stay motivated and prayed up. God loves you!

Sincerely,
Patricia Spratley

Introduction

In life, you will experience test and trials, but the one thing that I have learned is that with each test - there is a lesson. If you study hard and remain focused, God will give you the wisdom to pass the test. You have to let go and let God be God all by Himself. I had to learn the hard way, but I am grateful that I am still learning and growing.

This book is dedicated to my beautiful daughter Alexis S., and my wonderful Mother who has been there for me when I couldn't find my way. I would like to say to anyone who feels that they cannot continue their journey - see the miracles and blessing instead of the dark and dangerous road.

Patricia "Juicey" Spratley

My Life as a Child
From the Heart of My Mother

My daughter, Patricia Joy Spratley, was born in Norfolk, VA to Mrs. And Mr. Joyce and Theodore Spratley. Her oldest brothers name is Punkin. When she was born into the world she brought me nothing but joy, so I had no other choice but make her middle name Joy. As Patricia was growing up, she didn't have a lot of friends because I didn't allow her to play with too many kids. My daughter was a very smart young lady and she loved gymnastics and cheerleading. When she was only six years old, she would have a yard full of girls - teaching them how to do flips and cheer.

As my daughter grew into a teenager she began to go to Sunday school.

Soon after that, she started singing in the choir. On one Saturday morning she began to walk around the neighborhood inviting kids to church for Sunday school. Soon after -her dad, brother and I joined the church.

The pastor's wife called my daughter, "missionary girl," because she was working for Christ. My daughter had a very good childhood as she was growing up. I'm so proud of her for continuing to keep God first and praising the Most High.

Sincerely,
Joyce Spratley

Chapter 1

Born in 1968, during a time that the world was recovering from one of the largest tragedies, my mother was going through one as well. My mother grew up in Washington, DC. I am not sure of how she ended up in Norfolk, Virginia. It is amazing how much we don't know about our parents, yet we find ourselves traveling a journey lost and unsure of who we really are.

I asked my mother how she ended up in Georgia and she told me that when she was in Virginia, there was this sailor that she would sneak and see. She said she would always get caught by my dad. When she got caught, it would lead to abuse, and my mom said that she was tired. So, she called her friend, Clara Foster, in Atlanta Georgia.

I was about eight or nine months old when my mother, brother and I moved to Atlanta. My mother thought she had escaped but a few weeks later my daddy came to live with us.

Daddy was not a fairytale that most girls dream of. I can't say that I was "daddy's little girl." Ted was his name. He stood 5'9 with curly hair and was so light skinned that he almost looked white. He always wore a cowboy hat and all I can remember is him fussing all the time. I can't recall one happy memory between daddy and me. He didn't work. Instead, he was a bootlegger and for those of you who want to know what that is - he was the local resident that would sell liquor and beer to the people in the neighborhood.

There was always something going on when we were growing up. My daddy loved my brother and whenever he wanted, he received. Me, on the other hand, daddy would never acknowledge my wants. That caused me to feel completely unwanted by him and I resented my brother a lot. All I wanted was a doll and my brother wanted expensive things like motorcycles. My mom would do whatever she had to get me what I wanted. Momma was always trying to make other people happy. I often think about how she sacrificed and still sacrifices for us to be happy.

I remember one time - daddy jumped on momma. She got tired and ran to the neighbor's house. Daddy was so hell bent on momma being under his control, he came down there with a shot gun and made us come home. Momma never left. She stayed with daddy until the Lord called him home.

Daddy was a very hard-headed man and suffered from diabetes. He wouldn't eat right and never gave up liquor. One day he stumped his toe which caused infection and he had to have both of his legs amputated. Momma said that he didn't want her to have to take care of him. A few weeks later he died.

I was sitting at home when momma called me and told me that daddy was gone. I was sad but frustrated at the same time because I knew that momma would be alone. Momma loved daddy and that was all I knew. I never got the chance to talk to daddy and tell him how I felt all those years. I wanted to know what it felt like to be daddy's little princess.

As men, you should cherish what God gives you. My daddy gave the world to my brother but left me to feel unsure of what a real man was. Yes, daddy took care of us, but he didn't do the one thing that I needed the most. He didn't love me unconditionally or plant the seeds of wisdom, self-worth, and security within me.

Nineteen eighty-nine was the year my daddy passed away. If I had the chance to tell my daddy how I really felt back then, I would tell him how much I loved him, cared for him, and miss him.

Chapter 2

When God has a plan for life, nothing and no one can stop it. Not even you! I learned that valuable lesson back in 1998. The dark and dangerous road that I traveled no longer had its grip on me. I felt a sense of freedom in the very same place that had sucked the life out of me for years. It was as if God caused the world to stand still as He reached His hand from heaven and began to peel away the layers of addiction, abuse, low esteem, and uncertainty.

On that day in 1998, my life changed and would never be the same. The night before, there was a piece of me that wanted to leave and get high. Instead, I decided to stay at home with my daughter. The strange thing was that she had so much peace. I believe that was God's way of restoring me.

For years, Pastor would tell me to keep praying and God would change things. I must admit there were times that I didn't believe those words. He would tell me to be patient and wait on God. God was not coming around fast enough. Pastor also gave me a few scriptures to read. Psalm 23, Psalm 100 and Isaiah 11:1-9. Although I couldn't see God working in my life, I kept on reading those scriptures and in 1998 my life was changed without my consent. God didn't ask me if I was ready or if I needed more time. No, He did it and I am so glad.

As I look back at that time in my life, I am so grateful. My life was a constant episode of highs and lows. I never imagined that I would endure some of the things that I did, but today I can say that I am blessed. I am reminded that God does not need our permission to step in and save us from the dangerous situations that we put ourselves in. As I look back, I am reminded of how blessed I am and how far He has brought me.

I went from being a drug addict to becoming a woman who knows and values her worth. Am I perfect? Absolutely not, I am real with myself. I still have urges and I still yearn to have the things that I had in the past, but I have grown to ignore those feelings and realize that enough was enough. I realized that I had no choice.

My Pastor had given me the key to freedom -reading and repeating Gods Word, even when I didn't believe them. Subconsciously, my flesh began to come into alignment with my spirit.

Chapter 3

I can recall the first time that I was introduced to crack. I was so in love with my high school sweet heart. He was a working man, but he had a dark secret. As it is said, what you do in the dark will come to the light. The one thing about the streets, is that the streets has plenty of people who talk. One day, a friend of mine told me about who I will call "Number One."

He was getting high in a house not too far from where I lived. I couldn't believe it, so I decided one day to pop up and he was there. I could tell that he was ashamed and didn't want me to be involved in his habit. But, what we think is love, will make you do some strange things. Instead of me walking away and leaving the situation, I decided to stick around and became curious. I ended up becoming addicted to crack. Now, I had snorted cocaine before, but crack was a different monster.

Crack made me feel as though I needed more and more of it. I would do anything to get it. If I could give any advice to anyone out there who is thinking of doing any type of drug - I would tell you to turn around and walk away. Never think that something other than

God can heal your pain. No matter how high you get; no matter how far you run - God will find you and make His best attempt to grab your attention so you can see that He has a plan for your life. It's up to you to heed the warning signs.

I was born and raised in Atlanta, Georgia. I graduated from Fredrick Douglas High School in 1986 and then went to cosmetology school and graduated in 1987.

I met a young man and two months later, I was introduced to cocaine. While working as a stylist, I took several breaks after each client to snort cocaine. One day, while styling a client's hair, I made a mistake and cut the top of her ear because I was so high. I was one of the top stylists in Atlanta, GA. I had a client who worked in a local strip club and that led to the start of my adult entertainment life. I tried to strip and do hair but couldn't get up early enough in the morning to start on my client's hair because I would be so high from the night before. My clients began to get tired of sitting around waiting on me, so they found a different stylist and three months later, my entire clientele was gone.

One day, I was sitting in a crack house and everyone around me was smoking dope except for me. The crack pipe passed around me four times but the fifth time, I grabbed it and started smoking. At the time, I was also drinking alcohol very heavily. In 1991, I met a drug dealer in the club, went home with him for two hundred dollars and a sack of cocaine.

I didn't know that this guy was a womanizer. The relationship with him was very abusive. I got pregnant by him and my daughter was born December 12, 1992. One night, I went to my mother's house and while getting out of the car my daughter's father jumped from behind a tree. He was dressed in all black. I stepped out and he ran up behind me and snatched my coat over my head. He beat me with his fist and blackened both of my eyes. Almost every day, I was getting beat up and abused.

He even made me have sex with his friends while we snorted cocaine and drank beer. If I decided that I didn't want to have sex with him or his homeboys, I would get beat up and or slapped.

I remember when I decided to leave and go out of town to do a rated X video. He didn't want me to go but I left anyway. I was gone for four days. When I got back, he came to pick me up from my mother's house. He asked me where I'd been, and I told him. He started driving very fast down the street and pulled into some apartments. He asked one of his friends to bring him his 9mm and he did just as he was told.

The guy asked, "what are you about to do with that?" His reply was, "I'm gonna shoot this bitch." I immediately jumped out of the car, he shot at me about twelve times but only one bullet hit me. He yelled that he was going to shoot me in my vagina so that I wouldn't show it to anyone else. He shot me, however, the bullet was two inches away from my vagina.

I was rushed to Grady Memorial Hospital. The doctors told me that the bullet hit me in my thigh. It went in and came out. I went to my mom's house and stayed there for about four months.

Chapter 4

After my womb healed, I went right back to him because I was very afraid that he would kill me. Two days later, I was riding with him in the car and he put a pistol to my head and made me get in the trunk of the car because he thought that I was cheating on him.

I can recall a time that I was over to a friend's house and she told him that I wasn't over there. Two hours later I called a cab. When the cab came, she and I were getting into the cab and he grabbed me. He hit me in the face with a baseball bat. He knocked out five of my teeth. He made me get in the car with him, took me home and beat me again. The following day we spent most of the day having sex and later that day, I went to work at the night club. When I got off work, my car was stalling and as a result, I got home 45 minutes late. He beat me and blackened my eyes again.

That last time was enough to drive me to the root doctor. The young ladies there told me that if I continued to stay with him, he was going to eventually kill me in my sleep. The ladies told me to get two pictures of him and some items that he'd worn, like socks or underwear. I was to dig three holes in the back yard, so I dug the holes. One of the pictures, I had to burn the front of his face and bury the picture face down. The other picture was face up in another hole. I buried the underwear in the third hole.

Seven days went by and he suddenly disappeared from my life - no call or anything. After that day I considered myself blessed to get out of that situation. I went back to church and I talked to my pastor Rev. Harold Mathews about it. I told him that I was tired of abusing and prostituting my body for drugs. He gave me a few bible verses to read and told me that he would pray for me.

On Christmas Day, my brother bought me some Reeboks and a new sweat suit and that very same night, I sold those items for a $5.00 hit of crack.

I went back to church and talked to my pastor and he told me to give it some time. He said that God was going to answer my prayers and to just be patient and wait on Him.

He may not come when you want Him, but He'll be there on time. Every night I read Psalm 23, Psalm 100 and 2 Timothy 1:7. By 1998, I was no longer abusing drugs, nor drinking alcohol or prostituting. The Lord took the taste of alcohol and drugs away from me.

Chapter 5

In 2001, I became sick and started to have blurred vision and cramping in the back of my legs. I was rushed to the emergency room and told that I was a diabetic and that I also had high blood pressure.

In 2011, I started having diarrhea and vomiting every morning. This happened for four straight weeks. I went to Emory Hospital on South Cobb Drive that Saturday. When I arrived, they ran all kinds of tests. So, my brother came to see me that Thursday and he asked the doctor what was wrong with me and the doctors' reply was - "we're still running tests." My brother told them that I know longer needed his services and checked me out of the hospital and checked me into Emory Hospital at the Midtown Atlanta location.

I remember being in the Intensive Care Unit and Dr. Fisher came to tell me that my kidneys were in failing status. I stayed in the hospital for four weeks and a catheter was placed inside of my chest. Two days later, I was on dialysis. This was something that I didn't enjoy, but deep down inside I knew that it had to be done. Every night before I went to bed, I wrote on some sticky notes and placed them in the bible. I always prayed to be healed from being a diabetic and that my blood pressure would get back to normal.

As the years went by, ninety percent of the time, while I had diabetes, my blood sugar numbers were ranging anywhere from two hundred to five hundred. I went to visit my primary care physician and he told me that if I didn't get my blood sugar under control, I would end up blind with kidney failure. My Nephrologist placed me on the list to be evaluated for a kidney transplant. I went to the evaluation and the doctors told me that everything went well and that I had to wait on a call from the dialysis clinic.

I kept my regular dialysis clinic appointments every Thursday and Saturday. On February 1, 2013, I received a phone call from the transplant center saying that I had been placed on the standby list. I began to think, "what does that mean?" On that night before going to bed, I read Psalm 23 and Psalm 27. I wrote on my sticky notes – Lord, please help me find a job soon. Lord, please help me financially, Lord, please help my family and last, but not least – Lord, please send me a kidney.

On Feb 2, 2013, I was taking a shower when the phone began to ring. I rushed to answer it. A young lady said, "hello, may I speak to Patricia Spratley? My name is Dawn and I'm calling from The Emory Transplant Center. I just called a young man and told him that we had a kidney for him and he didn't want it. I'm calling you to see if you would like the kidney?"

My reply was "HELL YES." She proceeded to tell me that I needed to go the Emory Hospital on Clifton Road. I had to be there by 6:30 a.m. I woke up the next morning, my daughter and I got dressed and arrived at Emory at 6:20 a.m. I must have looked pretty anxious because a young lady stopped and asked if I needed help? I told her that I received a phone call for a kidney transplant. She escorted me to the Emergency Room admissions area. She also told me that she had just left the Chapel because there were a lot of things going on in her life. She hugged me and started crying as she said, "you are blessed because a lot of people have to wait two to three years before they can receive a transplant." She asked me how long I'd been on the transplant list. I replied that I was only on the list for eight months. She told me that she worked on the ninth floor and that she would come to visit me.

They put me in a room on 7-G. My doctor came to see me and told me that I was getting more than a kidney. I was getting a pancreas as well. God answered all my prayers. I received a new kidney and I was cured from diabetes. I stayed in the hospital for a week. Right after discharge, I went to church to see my pastor. He was very glad to see me.

Chapter 6

As the months passed, someone stole my Yorkie named Polo. I prayed about it and placed it in my bible. I prayed for God to help get my dog back and promised that I wouldn't let him out of my eyesight. I called channel two news and they aired the incident that Friday. Saturday morning, I received two phone calls and met up with a lady who returned my dog to me.

In April of 2013, my daughter came home from college and I noticed that she was acting strange. She was acting like someone had put something into her drink or her weed. She used to walk the streets at night and bring different men into our home, while I was asleep. She would also talk back to me and start fights with me. One night, she left her keys inside the house, so I locked her out. Her dad called me to let me know that she was walking the streets at night on the wrong side of town, hopping in and out of cars. I went through this for four months. She dropped out of college and came back home to stay.

I talked to my Pastor and told him that there was something wrong with my daughter. I really couldn't understand what her problem was. He said that he would keep me in his prayers.

As time passed, I was awakened by loud music. I got up and went to her room but there was a chair under the door knob. I called her name. She was in the restroom with the lights out, burning candles.

I kept praying and asking God to help me figure out what was wrong with my baby. I found an organization to call called Mobile Crisis. They came by the house to talk to her. She was very rude to the people from the organization. They immediately made an appointment for her to see a psychiatrist.

We went there only to find out that her Medicaid was not active, and she didn't have any insurance. I took her to South Fulton hospital and they kept her. She was considered a ten - thirteen, which translates to a suicidal patient. She was kept for twenty-four hours. The next day she was admitted into a mental facility. She stayed on watch for two days. I picked her up after the two day stay; they prescribed her medication that kept her from hearing voices and helped her rest.

I tried to talk to her that day, but she was so defensive toward me. We got into a fight, she pushed me down and I broke my knee. I was taken to the emergency room and had to stay hospitalized for six weeks. Two months later she ran out of medication and I was unable to afford it. This particular medication cost one hundred and seventy-five dollars for thirty pills. I had no way of paying for this medicine, so I prayed hard and asked God to help me. My prayer was simple. I'm standing in the need of prayer and I'm coming to you today, Lord, because I have no one else to call on. Please help me find a way to get my daughter's medication as well as see the doctor. I finally found her some help and she was able to see a doctor. He wrote a prescription for her medication. Now her medication and doctor visits are free.

You can't tell me that the God that I serve is not an awesome God. He's so worthy to be praised!

Chapter 7

Freak Nick ATL

I was invited to a party at a five-star hotel downtown. There were five strippers and twenty guys. At this party, we prostituted, snorted cocaine and drank alcohol. We'd stayed up for about two days just getting high. Within seconds, I collapsed and had a seizure. They ran out of the room and dialed 911.

I awakened to the sound of doctors trying to talk to me. They asked me all kinds of questions that I couldn't respond to because I didn't remember. Now, I suffer from a seizure disorder. This was caused by abusing drugs, and from being hit upside the head by my child's father.

Club Scene

I was on stage one night dancing and when my second song started, I began to feel strange. I ran really fast off the stage and started running water on my face. The next thing I knew, I was at the emergency room again with doctor's asking me questions like - what's my name, what was the date and who was he president? I couldn't remember anything. I told them that the president was

Abraham Lincoln. I couldn't even remember who I was or the date of the month.

I met a guy while dancing in the club who fell deeply in love with me and began a relationship with him. This guy liked me for who I was, and he didn't care about my past. He bought me a car and found an apartment for me and my daughter to live in. I was with him for nine years. During the tenth year, I found someone else. A younger guy that I was physically attracted to and I invited him to my home to have sex with him. Pretty soon, I began to fall in love with the younger guy. Shortly after that, he began to drain me financially because I was giving him my money and providing transportation for him.

I tried to be committed to them both but soon I began taking the old man's money and giving it to the young guy. This went on until I finally got caught by the older gentleman. He got so upset and took the car that he paid for and made me move out of the house. I lost everything I had in the blink of an eye.

I now understand why the bible says, "Pray for those that despitefully use you." After that, my life started into a downward spiral. I prayed and asked God for forgiveness and He blessed me with a job. I was working in an adult entertainment club as a manager earning two to five hundred dollars a night, six days a week. I bought another car and moved into a luxury apartment.

After working at the club for about eight years, I began to notice that one of the supervisors didn't really care for me because I wouldn't date him. Going into my ninth year, he called me into the office on a Friday night and told me that he didn't need me anymore.

I decided that I really needed to change my profession. So, I went back to school to start a career in pharmaceutical technology. I went to school for eight months and graduated with honors. Soon after, I went on several job interviews and still hadn't found work. During that time, I went to a total of seventeen job interviews.

Chapter 8

My Church Days

I joined a Baptist church on the westside of Atlanta when I was eight years old. I was one of the lead singers in the choir. My brother and dad came to church to hear me sing.

When I got older, I joined the gospel chorus and became one of the lead singers in that choir as well. The songs that I sing are all about the things that I have gone through in life. Singing really helps me to release all the stress and pain that I experience on a regular basis. I can tell when the Spirit hits me because I am so happy!

In 2012, I decided to change my membership to my daughter's church. The Pastor was awesome. He often preached about the things that I overcame and was going through and it really blessed me. The church took me in with open arms and embraced me with love as I shared my testimony and all the obstacles that I overcame. I also received an award for the Best Women's Overcomer of The Year from my Pastor.

My Experience with Broken Bones

In September of 2013, I was in a tussle with my best friend. She pushed me down and broke my knee. I couldn't apply pressure to my knee for two months. On January 26, 2014, I was headed out of the house on the way to church. I was walking down the steps and noticed that there was a crack at the bottom of the steps; and I tumbled down and fell on my ankle. I didn't realize it at the time, but it was broken. After going to church and still not feeling well, I went to the emergency room and the nursing staff did an x-ray. That's when they informed me that my ankle was broken.

I asked God, "What are you trying to tell me? Do I need to sit down and wait on you? Am I moving too fast Lord?" The Lord will make a way out of no way. I realized that I had to stop telling God about my problems and start telling my problems about my God.

The Devil Is A Lie

I was admitted into the hospital on July 2, 2018, for a persistent cough that I'd had for some time. Doctors really didn't know where the cough was coming from. So, I told them about a young lady that worked in an Adult Entertainment Club with me. She had this same cough so we all were checked for tuberculosis. I was tested and had to take meds for this since the cough had returned.

The staff couldn't tell me what was wrong with me, but they put me isolation until they could run some more test and get some results. I was treated very poorly while there and had to eat cold food! They said that "once my food is airborne it couldn't be taken out of room." I was really pissed off because I knew that I was being treated differently from all the other patients on this floor. I began reading Psalm 1:1-6 and it helped me to understand the things that I was dealing with.

These are my miracles and blessings from Almighty God!

In God We Trust

Today is another chapter of my life. I've learned not to trust anybody but GOD. There was a young lady that I met through a high school friend who was supposed to do something for me. I was disappointed because she decided to back out and not do it. It took her four years to decide that she didn't want to be the publisher of my book. This is how God showed me that she wasn't the right person for this venture in my life.

Putting my faith and trust in God is what keeps me from getting depressed, emotional, frustrated and just out right mad!

Lord, I want to thank You, for everything that you are showing me right now, in the name of Jesus.

About the Author

Ms. Patricia Spratley was born in Norfolk, Virginia. She moved to Atlanta, Georgia at the age of 8 and has resided there since. Patricia graduated from Frederick Douglas High School in 1986. From there, she attended cosmetology school and became a hair stylist.

She developed a drug addiction. She became a victim of an abusive relationship. Ms. Spratley began to live a racy, toxic lifestyle. Later, she was diagnosed with kidney failure along with diabetes and hypertension.

Ultimately, Ms. Spratley gave her life to Christ. She has been clean from drugs for 17 years. She recently graduated from pharmacy technician school with honors.

In February of 2013, Ms. Spratley received a kidney and pancreas transplant. She has been off dialysis and insulin ever since.

Patricia is also the author of miracles and Blessings, sharing her life experiences to inspire others.

Made in the USA
Monee, IL
11 April 2022